ONE MONSTER AFTER ANOTHER

BY MERCER MAYER

For Zebulon,

I love you

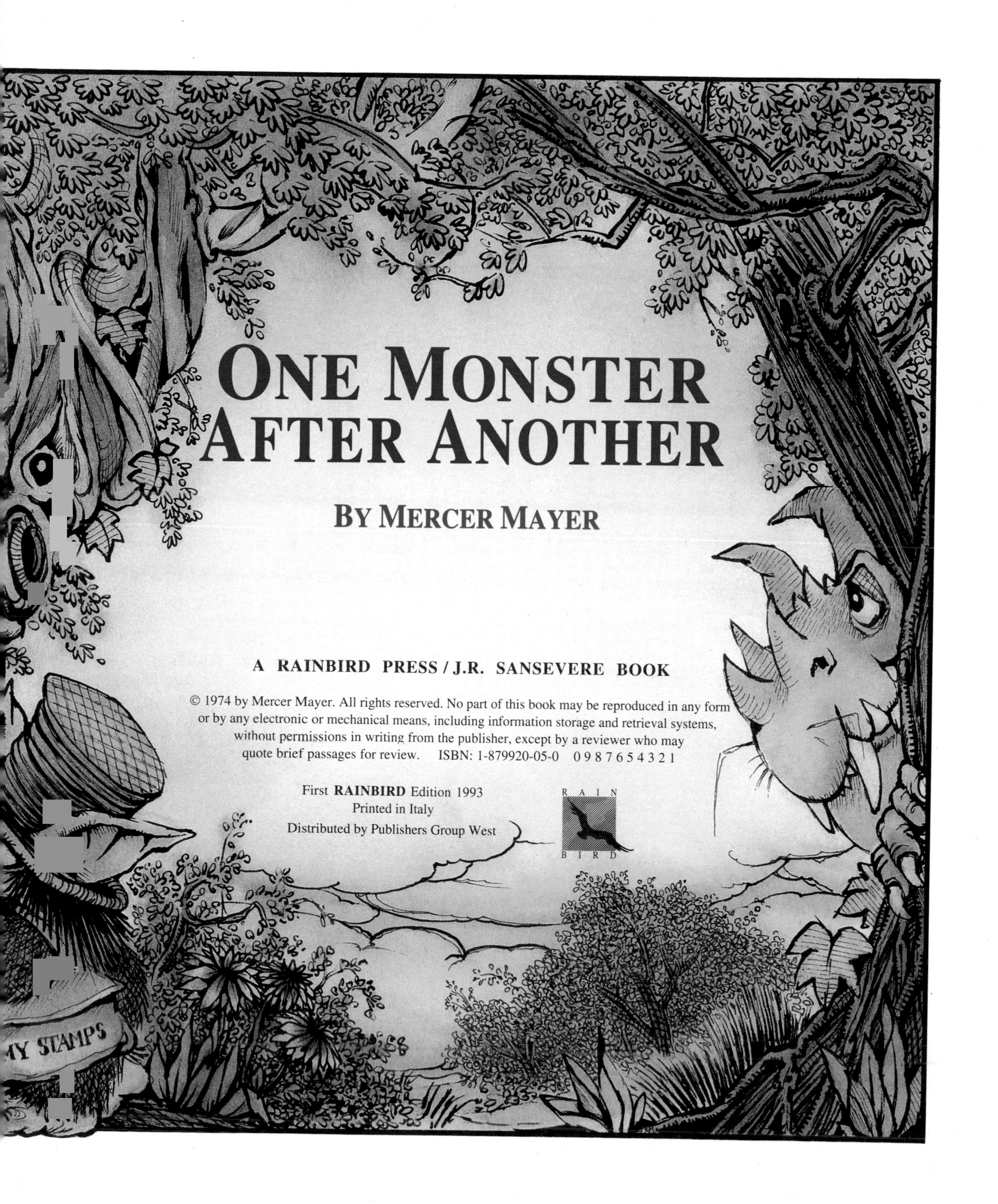

ONE MONSTER AFTER ANOTHER

BY MERCER MAYER

A RAINBIRD PRESS / J.R. SANSEVERE BOOK

 ISBN: 1-879920-05-0 0 9 8 7 6 5 4 3 2 1

First **RAINBIRD** Edition 1993
Printed in Italy
Distributed by Publishers Group West

RAIN
BIRD

One day Sally Ann wrote a letter to her best friend Lucy Jane. She put it in an envelope and put the envelope into her mailbox.

219
FADDLE ST.
MY STAMPS

U.S.
MAIL
219
FADDLE ST.

But before the mailman came, a Stamp-Collecting Trollusk crept up to the mailbox, stole the letter, and gabbled away with a smirk on his snerk.

TO NOWHERE
and
BACKAGAIN

But before the Stamp-Collecting Trollusk could tear off the stamp and collect it, a Letter-Eating Bombanat flew out of Nowhere and snapped up the letter.

Over the Blue Ocean of Bubbly Goo the Letter-Eating Bombanat flew.

But before he could find a nice place to settle down and eat the letter, a Bombanat-Munching Grumley reached up out of the goo and grabbed him.

But before the Bombanat-Munching Grumley could slither down into the sea for a nice Bombanat lunch–SNAP–he was snagged by a big fishing net and hauled wiggly-squiggly on board a fishing boat.

But before the fishing boat could reach land, it was struck by a Furious-Floating Ice-Ferg. SCRUNNCCCHHH!! As the ship went down, the captain quickly stuffed a note into a bottle. He pushed in the letter for good measure, and then threw it into the ocean.

But before anyone could find the bottle, a Wild-'n-Windy Typhoonigator came storming along, sucking up everything in its path. It sucked up the whole Blue Ocean of Bubbly Goo–the bottle, too–then blew itself away.

GARBY'S GARAGE
YOU BREAK IT • WE FIX IT.

By morning, the Wild-'n-Windy Typhoonigator was full, so full of fishing boats, bottles, and bubbly goo, that it had to let go.

Down fell the letter which was in the bottle which was in the Blue Ocean of Bubbly Goo. Down fell the bottle, KER-PLOP, right on the head of a Paper-Munching Yalapappus who lived on the edge of Nowhere.
The bottle broke, tinkle-plinkle, and out fell the Captain's note and the letter. The Yalapappus smiled. It had been such a long time since he'd had any nice paper to munch.

Gleefully he grabbed the Captain's note and munched it. But before he could munch the letter, too, the Stamp-Collecting Trollusk, who just happened to be passing by, snatched the letter in his snerk and ran away.

The Paper-Munching Yalapappus trundled after him, shouting and loudly grimming.

MY STAMPS

Suddenly, out of the sky swooped the Letter-Eating Bombanat. SNIP! He snapped up the letter.

But before the Letter-Eating Bombanat could eat the letter, he was snared in a net, caught, FLIP-FLOP, by the Bombanat-Collecting Grithix.

The Grithix, as everybody knows, is a Bombanat collector, not a letter collector. He had no use for someone else's mail, so he did what anybody should do with a lost letter. He mailed it! The Paper-Munching Yalapappus and the Stamp-Collecting Trollusk and the Letter-Eating Bombanat watched helplessly as the Grithix opened an official-looking mailbox and dropped the letter in.

Sally Ann

OVERTHERE
EITHER WAY
RIGHTHERE
MAILBOX

And before they could steal the mailbox, a mailman rode up on an official-looking motorcycle.

"Stop!" he cried. "Unhand that official mailbox!"

There was nothing they could do. After all, he was an official mailman.

The official mailman opened the official mailbox and took out all the letters. Away he rode, leaving the Yalapappus and the Trollusk waving their paws in the air and wailing at the Bombanat-Collecting Grithix.

The Grithix didn't care a snickle. Paying no attention to all the noise, he walked home, clasping the Letter-Eating Bombanat firmly under one arm.

LAST STOP FOR GAS
IF YOU ARE GOING
THAT WAY
A FREE 150lb. ALLIGATOR WITH EACH 10 GALLONS OF GAS
WHILE THEY LAST
WE ACCEPT ALL CREDIT CARDS
COUNTRY STORE
GIFTS
GAS
FREE GAS
WITH EACH
GIFT
YOU BUY

To THE EDGE OF NOWHERE
WHILE YOU ARE THERE
HAVE A
BURGER
AT
PETE'S PLACE
STAMPS
END OF
PAVEMENT

FIRST CLASS
75

hen Lucy Jane opened her mailbox that afternoon, inside was the letter from Sally Ann.

Dear Lucy Jane,
Nothing exciting ever happens around here.
Please come and visit.
Your Best Friend,
Sally Ann

75
MAIL

MY STAMPS

MERCER MAYER was born in Little Rock, Arkansas, and grew up in Hawaii. He studied at the Honolulu Academy of Art and the Art Students League in New York City. He is the author-illustrator of many children's books, including *What Do You Do with a Kangaroo?*, winner of the Brooklyn Art Books for Children Citation; *Liza Lou and the Yeller Belly Swamp; The Wizard Comes to Town;* and *You're the Scaredy-Cat.* Among the many books he has illustrated are *Beauty and the Beast;* and *Everyone Knows What a Dragon Looks Like,* winner of the 1976 Irma Simonton Black Award and named one of the nine best illustrated children's books of the year by *The New York Times.* Mr. Mayer is also the creator of the best-selling Little Critter® series.

He and his wife Gina live and work together at their home in Connecticut.